Douglas Lindsay was born in Scotland in 1964, in the middle of the night. Contrary to earlier reports, the weather was fine.

He conceived the character of Barney Thomson while living in Senegal, West Africa. He now lives in the Highlands of Scotland, with his wife and two children.

Barney Thomson &
The Face of Death

Douglas Lindsay

Long Midnight Publishing

This edition published in Great Britain in 2002 by
Long Midnight Publishing
Suite 433
24 Station Square
Inverness IV1 1LD
e-mail: info@barney-thomson.com

www.barney-thomson.com

*A catalogue record for this book is available
from the British Library*

ISBN: 0 9541387 0 8

Manufacture co-ordinated by
Book-In-Hand Ltd, London

For Jessica & Hamish

Acknowledgements

The author would like to thank the following for their assistance: Kathryn, Jessica, Hamish, Donald, Anita & Lesley.

He also wishes to acknowledge the contribution of *Ross & Cromarty Enterprise*, without whom this book would not have been produced.

CONTENTS

Prologue

The Usual 'Four Guys Go Off
Into The Woods And Die' Thing

"The woods decay, the woods decay and fall,
The vapours weep their burthen to the ground,
Something about fields and that kind of stuff,
And a bit about a swan dying..."
Alfred Lord Tennyson (1809-92)

It was a cold day in the middle of January, when four young men walked into the Blackmuir Wood above the Victorian Spa village of Strathpeffer, sixteen miles west of Inverness, in the Highlands of Scotland. They were from the town of West Warwick, Rhode Island, and were in the middle of their gap year between High School and Boston College. They had travelled four months in Asia, and had only arrived in Europe two days earlier. They intended doing Britain and France, before going on through Switzerland to Italy. If they had the time, they thought they might try to reach North Africa. They were, however, destined never to get beyond the Blackmuir Wood above Strathpeffer.

When, on that Friday afternoon, they failed to emerge from the wood, their disappearance was not noted, as they had informed no one of their plans. Two days later, however,

13

their bodies were discovered by a young couple, near the Touchstone Maze in the middle of the forest. The throats of all four men had been slit. The instrument of their deaths, an old pair of barber scissors, had been left beside them, still stained with four different types of blood. And a mixture of those four different types of blood had been used to draw a crude picture on the side of the standing stone nearest to where the bodies had been left. A clumsily etched depiction of an Obi Wan type hood, drawn back from a thin and haunted face. A face with sockets without eyes, and a mouth open in howling lament. A face that would wail for all eternity.

The men were fully clothed and, as far as anyone could tell, none of their possessions had been taken. There was no sign of a struggle, no clue whatsoever to the events that had led to their murder.

There was one peculiarity, however, about the four bodies. Each of the men, before he had died, had been given the most frighteningly awful haircut.

1

Barney Strolled Into Town, And Booked Himself A Room In The Local Saloon

"The seaman tells stories of winds, the ploughman
of bulls; the soldier details his wounds;
the barber talks a complete load of pants."
Propertius (50-16BC)

There are two kinds of people in the world.

There are those who have never accidentally murdered their work colleagues, discovered their mother is a serial killer, had to dispose of eight bodies, gone on the run from the police, hidden out in a monastery where the monks were murdered one by one, killed the monastery murderer, and been allowed to walk free by the two investigating officers at the scene of the crimes.

And those who have…

f

Barney Thomson walked into the small town of Strathpeffer at four o'clock in the afternoon. It was a little over three weeks since he had left the monastery of the Holy Order of the Monks of St. John. He'd done a lot of walking, and a lot of thinking. However, while his legs were turning into those of a honed athlete, his mind was turning into that of one of the lower invertebrates. So he had stopped thinking. From now on it would be his destiny to walk the Earth and get in adventures, meeting whatever came his way with a ready quip, a steely eye and a robust pair of bollocks. Nothing was going to faze him.

He came into town on the Contin road, with the housing estates on his left. Down the hill past the churches and into the centre of the town, where the old pavilion slowly crumbled in sad dilapidation, and every second building was a hotel.

Strathpeffer reached its peak at the turn of the twentieth century when the Victorians came to bathe in the crystal clear, sub-zero waters. A branch line was added to the railway, hotels sprang up like cactus in the Arizona desert, and the local Highlanders mingled with royalty and the cream of London society in a wondrously eclectic mix. The Strathpeffer Gazette reported on the seventeenth of August 1893, that '*after bathing splendidly in the most glorious of cold waters for a matter of some three hours, Her Majesty Queen Victoria, 70, emerged so invigorated, that she robustly fornicated with seven unwieldy but handsome Scotsmen, being rodgered vigorously between the buttocks, and performing heartily and with the utmost gusto in a variety of the most singular positions, for what could only be described as thirty to forty minutes.*'

As the years had passed, and the majority of people heading north to cure themselves of all manner of aches and pains had failed to be cured, the cream of London society had drifted away, the pump room and pavilion had drifted to ruin, and only the hotels—some eight or nine hundred of them—had remained, to cater for the Highland tourist industry.

Barney booked himself into a room in the Highland Inn. He had little money, but had decided to treat himself to a night with a decent roof over his head, a couple of drinks and a proper meal. He exchanged a few words with the desk clerk—dressed in black—carried his small bag up the stairs to the room, let himself in and collapsed onto the bed, where he fell into the sort of troubled sleep which he'd been having for some weeks.

He would dream of long and strange conversations with serial killers, where he himself would be a murderer, talking frankly of his victims, and how he intended adding to his collection. And he would always awake troubled and tired and wondering if it was to be his destiny to become the man of his nightmares.

f

That evening, the day that the bodies of the American students had been discovered, Barney walked into the bar of the hotel, plonked himself on a stool and stared glumly up at the vast array of whiskies on offer. He only had money for one or two drinks, and he could have done with a couple of shots. But it would have to be lager, so that he would have a decent sized drink to spin out over the course of the evening.

'What can I get you?' asked the barman, having just served a young couple with a brace of depressingly sterile vodka mixers, the type of drinks that ad men everywhere like to imply are seriously cool to drink.

'Lager, please,' said Barney.

'No bother,' said the barman, a rough looking chap with a cream cheese face and ears which had been flattened out using a workbench tool constructed of some sturdy metal. He poured the drink; Barney watched as the smooth golden brown fluid filled the glass.

'You're looking a bit miserable there,' said the barman, who was called Bobby, as a conversational opener. It was a slow night and he needed the crack.

'Thanks,' said Barney. 'You're looking fine yourself.'

'Oh, thanks,' said Bobby, missing the sarcasm. 'You've noticed my complexion?'

Barney looked across the bar, as the pint was handed over. Only in the most virulent cases of psoriasis do men notice the complexion of other men.

'Aye,' said Barney, dourly, not knowing what else to say, and wondering if he was about to be propositioned.

'Aye,' said Bobby, stroking his cheek, 'I've been drinking my own pish. It does wonders for it.'

Barney stared at the light golden brown liquid from which he was about to take his first sip.

'First thing in the morning,' said Bobby, 'when it's fresh and warm and steaming. Absolutely brilliant for the skin. You should try it.'

Barney didn't answer. He was still staring at his lager.

'Any other time of the day, and it's lost all its goodness. Has to be first thing,' said Bobby. 'Course,' he continued, 'there's the question of what to do if you need to take a pish in the middle of the night. Opinion is divided in the scientific community.'

'Aye,' said Barney, 'I saw that on the Discovery Channel.'

And finally he delved into his lager and took a long slow drink, his first alcohol in some weeks, and he could feel the cold liquid pour down his throat and through his chest and into his stomach. It tasted smooth and glorious and mellow, and was like taking a first wonderful breath of fresh air.

'Did you know that every one of us has eight pounds of undigested meat in his colon?' said Bobby. 'Apart from veggies, of course. They've got eight pounds of carrots or chocolate or something up there. But, I mean, eight pounds?'

Barney nodded. He took another drink, shorter this time, savouring the taste, trying to ignore Bobby the barman.

'That's like, what, a stone or something?' said Bobby, shaking his head. 'That's why I'm about to go for that collonic irrigation thing, you know. A quick swoosh up the arse with a jet of water, or whatever it is they use. How hard can that be, eh?'

Barney nodded. Might as well go for it. Literally talking pish. What the Hell.

'I've heard they do it with a pink milk shake type fluid,' said Barney.

'No, that's an enema,' said Bobby. 'Or strawberry milk shake, that's a pink milk shake type fluid. No, for collonic irrigation they use lighter fluid or kerosene or something.'

'I don't think they put a match to it or anything, though,' he added as an afterthought.

'That's tremendous,' said Barney. 'I'm really pleased for you.'

'Thanks,' said Bobby. 'I'll be getting the women, no end. There'll be a queue from here to Ullapool.'

'Aye,' said Barney.

'The Age of Bobby The Barman is coming,' said Bobby the barman.

'What's your chat up line going to be?' asked Barney. 'Fancy a shag love. My back passage has been vacuumed and you should taste my pish. Good length, with hints of citrusy fruits.'

'I might just use that,' said Bobby, smiling.

And they lapsed into silence. Bobby found a couple of glasses to dry, doing that barman thing, while Barney delved long and hard into the lager that was supposed to sustain him half the evening, so that after three and a half minutes it was almost finished.

'You'll have heard about those four tourists they found?' asked Bobby, after a while, the silence beginning to bother him.

No reason for it, but the soft voice with the barest trace of a Highland accent, the voice that did not go with the fairly repellent exterior, cut into Barney's feeling of ease. Suddenly he felt a shiver course through his body, an ugly shiver which left a vicious feeling of discomfort. He closed his eyes momentarily, and in the darkness he saw four bodies lying in a forest, their throats slit. And on the standing stone behind, he saw the face drawn in blood, and it stared at him in its perpetual terror.

His eyes shot open again. He looked at Bobby the barman, and it seemed as if he'd had his eyes closed for several minutes. The vision had left him with goosebumps across his body, the small hairs at the back of his neck standing upright, the colour drained from his cheeks.

'You all right?' said Bobby.

'Aye,' said Barney, 'aye. Four tourists?' he asked quickly, thinking that he might as well get it over with.

'Americans,' said Bobby. 'Found them up at the stone circle. There was a young couple dived off into the woods —between you and me, it was that Mhairi Henderson, but that's a secret now, 'cause her mother still thinks she's seeing wee David, you know Mrs Jackson's boy. But the thing is, she split with him about three weeks ago after she met Alec Fairburn, and you know what they say about him. Which is why Mrs Henderson wouldn't be too chuffed to hear that he was on the verge of giving her daughter a good seeing to. Not after all that business with Fiona and Beattie at Sophie's wedding, if you know what I mean.'

The goosebumps had died away, to be replaced by resignation bumps. Forlorn bumps, where his skin, along with the rest of his body, sadly accepted that Barney's place in life was to listen to other men talk an endless stream of drivel; and to consistently find himself in towns with a prodigious murder rate.

'The four Americans?' said Barney.

'Throats slit,' said Bobby. 'With a pair of scissors.'

Barney nodded. That was hardly a surprise.

'Apparently they'd each been given a bit of a shocker of

20

a haircut before they'd been killed,' said Bobby.

I know all about that, thought Barney, but he didn't say anything. No point in turning himself into the number one suspect within two minutes of arriving in town.

'How d'you mean?' asked Barney. 'Was the style a shocker, even though it'd been well executed by the barber, or was it your actual bad bit of hairdressing?'

Bobby nodded.

'You sound like you know what you're talking about?' he said, eyeing Barney with appreciation.

'Obvious question,' said Barney, shrugging.

'Normal haircuts, gone wrong,' said Bobby, and he leant across the bar, drawing Barney into his confidence. 'They're saying that it looked like one guy was supposed to have been given a regulation Sinatra '62…you're familiar with it?'

'Aye,' said Barney.

'It was so bad, he looked like Lana Turner,' said Bobby, raising an eyebrow.

'Tragedy,' said Barney. Then he added, 'You seem to be very well informed.'

'I'm a barman,' said Bobby.

And Barney nodded and thought that bartending wasn't that different from barbering or taxi driving or being a priest or a psychologist. You always ended up with more information than you might reasonably be expected to know.

'They're saying that Barney Thomson did it,' said the barman.

Barney nodded. Of course they are.

'Nah,' said Barney, 'he had the Sinatra '62 down pat.'

Bobby the barman nodded.

'You might be right,' he said, sagely. 'Maybe it was one of his accomplices.'

Barney Thomson himself nodded, polished off his pint

and wondered just who exactly his accomplices were supposed to be. And the fact that if he had any, the first thing he'd do would be to teach them the Sinatra '62.

2

Here They Come,
Walking Down The Street

"And I looked, and behold a pale horse:
and his name that sat on him was Death,
And Hell followed with him, saying:
A be bop a loo bop, a lop bam boom."
Book of Revelations ch.6 v.8

Federal Agents arrived in the Highlands the following day. Legal Attachés Damien Crow and Lara Cameron, the FBI's representatives in London, England, had been granted authority to become involved in the investigation. Well out of their remit, but the horrible nature of the crime and the uproar that it had caused in their homeland—it'd been a slow news day, with even the Ravens' pasting at the hands of the Broncos making the front page of the New York Times— had led the ambassador in London to seek immediate representation to have two of his officers included in the case.

And so they arrived in Strathpeffer at 1015hrs and by the type of strange coincidence that now seemed to be haunting Barney Thomson's life, they booked into the Highland Inn. Crow was tall and thin, his face vaguely reminiscent of Hoagy Carmichael, his hair shaved brutally close to the scalp, his eyes dark and sombre. Cameron was a massively attractive woman, robustly built, full buttocked and breasted, lips that could suck a basketball through a straw, blonde hair cut in a lovely bob that circled her face, and tremendously erotic feet, if you're into that sort of thing. (And a lot of people are, if the guys who run the foot fetish websites are to be believed.)

When they walked into the hotel reception to check in, each carrying a small bag, Detective Sergeant McLeod behind them, his gaze curiously drawn to Cameron's black and tan DMs, Barney was sitting not ten yards away reading that morning's Scotsman, the headline of which detailed the latest mass murder. *Four Dead As Thomson Switches To Ethnic Cleansing.* Already he had made up his mind that he could not face the thought of stepping out into another cold day, and was going to stay an extra night in the hotel, thereby stretching his budget to the death.

Crow thumped his hand on the bell and a small woman, bereft of composure, hurried out from the inner office and looked at the three new arrivals with a vague air of panic.

'Hello,' she said, her voice a beautiful Highland lilt.

'Damien Crow,' said Crow.

'Lara Cameron,' said Cameron. 'My family left Scotland in 1643,' she added.

'Did they?' said Rhona McAndrew. 'Very nice.'

'I've still got a cousin in Falkirk. You know her?' said Cameron.

McAndrew stared at her for a few seconds, looked at Sergeant McLeod and turned back to Cameron.

'Your office called this morning. You're in adjacent rooms,' she said, ignoring the Falkirk thing. 'If you'd like to sign here, I'll get someone to show you up.'

'That's all right, ma'am,' said Crow, 'we'll find it.'

Their accents had attracted Barney's interest. He looked up from the report in the paper—*Local crimper Luke McGowan,*

47, said he was astonished by the shocking haircuts which had been given to the four victims, prior to their murder. 'Barbery as horrifying as this, destabilises the very infrastructure of humanity,' he claimed, as he stood in his shop distributing complex cuts such as the Wittgenstein and the Bradley Whitford '97—and studied Cameron and Crow.

Four Americans had been murdered, now there were two more Americans newly arrived in town, reeking of authority, looking as if they were about to embark on some police action or other. The connection was obvious, and the first thing they would be told when they'd stepped off the plane was that the man they were looking for was Barney Thomson.

He was still staring at them, as they took their keys from Mrs McAndrew and turned and headed towards the stairs. As they walked past him, Crow was looking at the stag's head above the staircase, staring down dourly—although of course it was dour, it'd been shot—at all who passed beneath it. Cameron, however, caught Barney's eye. Strangely for Barney, he recognised the attractiveness of her. Perhaps it was that which stopped him drawing his eyes away from her, but they held each other's gaze, as she walked by no more than ten feet away.

She stopped, as Crow passed under the gloomy stag. Barney felt a little flutter in his stomach, but after all that he had been through in the previous year, really this was no big thing. Only a woman, and why should he get nervous about that? Well, that and the fact that she was a policewoman with the obvious potential to arrest him and send him to prison for the rest of his life.

'Hi,' she said. 'Beautiful country.'

'Thanks,' said Barney. And he kind of smiled, but it very probably came across wrong.

'My family left here in 1643,' she said. 'My name's Cameron.'

'Right,' said Barney. 'They lived in Strathpeffer?'

She laughed at herself, and Barney tried not to stare at her lips, because he found them so attractive.

'No, just Scotland, you know. My cousin still lives in Falkirk. Do you know her?'

'Em,' said Barney, thinking the obvious, but not wanting to say it, 'I, eh, you know,' was all he managed to say over the following few seconds. 'Never been to Falkirk,' he ejaculated eventually.

'That's a shame,' she said. And they stared at each other, and neither had anything else to say. Barney, for reasons he wasn't quite sure of, was trying desperately to think of something, but he could have sat there for another three or four million years and not thought of anything that wouldn't have made him sound like a complete and utter loony.

And so eventually she smiled and nodded and turned and followed Legal Attaché Damien Crow under the dead stag and on up the stairs.

Barney watched the space where she had been for a few seconds then looked back at the paper. *Profile Of Man Who Holds Entire Planet In Grip Of Fear*, was the headline above an article about himself, and he stared at it curiously, still thinking about Attaché Cameron.

'She fancies you,' said a voice to his right.

He looked over. There was a guy in a suit reading the Daily Telegraph.

'What?' said Barney.

'Hi,' said the man. 'Here's my card.' And he stretched forward and handed Barney his calling card. Theodore Wolf, Marketing Consultant. Barney stared at it, until he realised he was supposed to take it from him, took it and quickly put it in his pocket.

'That's nice,' said Barney.

'No, seriously,' said Wolf. 'She was into your pants big

style. I'd watch her friend, mind you, 'cause he looked like a serial killer.'

Barney nodded. Wolf stared at him.

'Why,' said Wolf, 'as a woodcock to mine own springe, Osric; I am justly killed with my own treachery.'

'What?' said Barney.

'Hamlet,' said Wolf.

Barney looked blankly at him. Why couldn't people just not talk shite? How difficult is it to not talk shite in this day and age?

'It may well be,' said Barney, deciding to take him to task, 'but is it relevant in even the remotest way to what we were talking about?'

'Not really,' said Wolf, after a pause. He was used to people being intimidated and thinking him deep when he quoted Shakespeare.

'Well, shut up, then,' said Barney. 'You ever met a serial killer anyway?' he added.

Wolf laughed, a laugh which died on his lips when he saw the look in Barney's eyes. Being a marketing consultant, he conceptualised several things to say, but strangely thought the better of all of them. So he slowly lifted the paper in order that Barney was obscured, buried his head, and tried to concentrate on the story of Geri Halliwell's breast reduction.

And when Wolf glanced nervously round the paper a few seconds later, to check to see if the man with the weird glint in his eye was about to draw a chainsaw out of his back pocket and noisily cleave his head off, Barney was gone.

f

Crow drove the 4x4 up the forest track, round the top and down into the centre of the wood to where the four bodies had been discovered next to the Touchstone Maze. He stepped out of the vehicle with Cameron and McLeod and into the cold early afternoon. The pale sun was already heading towards the mountains in the west faster than a Louisiana dog into a lizard pit, and the temperature was falling to somewhere just below zero—where it was pretty much destined to remain until sometime in the middle of August.

There was one other police car there. The area had been sealed off and was being attended by two officers. Along the north-west boundary of the clearing where the concentric stone circles had been built, was a stone wall bordering farmland, with a view out over the town and Ben Wyvis rising behind. The rest of the clearing was surrounded by forest.

The three of them stood together looking up at the mountain and then at their immediate surroundings. The labyrinth was not large, most of the stones no more than four or five feet high. There were eighty-one of them, lain in five concentric circles, leading to the vortex at the centre. Well perhaps, not so much of a vortex, as a bit of a space.

'How long's this been here?' said Crow, assuming several thousand years and no end of conspiracy theories about aliens as to its construction.

'A few years,' said McLeod.

'Right.'

'It was based on an ancient labyrinth design of prehistoric origin. The earliest records of labyrinths in Scotland are from Pictish and Celtic rock carvings.'

'Right,' said Crow.

'The stones were taken from around Scotland, you know, you've got all sorts here. Like the stones from the Outer Hebrides which were formed around three billion years ago. That's, like, a really long time.'

'Yep,' said Crow, trying to think of a way to extricate himself from the conversation.

'Then there's the youngest Highland rock which was

formed in the Jurassic. There's metamorphosed limestone, mica schist with granite pegmatite veins, there's granodiorites with layering, possibly caused by fractioned crystallisation or dissolution of country rock…'

He looked at Crow who was showing him the palm of his hand.

'What?' said McLeod.

'You're boring me,' said Crow.

'Oh,' said McLeod. 'All right, then.'

'Good,' said Crow, his thoughts already moving on. He'd been in Britain for eight months and was still coming to terms with the fact that not everything in the country was two thousand years old. Just the rail network and the attitude to foreigners.

He walked through the stones, running his fingers across them as he passed by, leaving the job of finding out about the project to Cameron, who was reading the information boards at the head of labyrinth.

He worked his way round until he reached the stone which had been marked up with the ghoulish face. He bent down and studied it more closely, then turned and walked back towards McLeod.

'Know of any specific connection between the circle and the victims?' said Crow. They were beside an area that had been further cordoned off, and was guarded by two officers.

McLeod shrugged.

'They're right next to each other,' he said.

'Not what I meant, cowboy,' said Crow. 'Why here?' he added, pointing into the woods.

'No connection,' said McLeod 'He took the four guys up into the wood, no idea how he managed to get them to go, then he cut their hair and slit their throats. Very nasty.'

'Did he do the haircutting up here, or someplace else?'

They were now standing in front of Constables Garvie

and McIntosh, two men who looked very cold, despite their large and thick jackets.

'Someplace else, we think,' said McLeod.

'Aye,' said Garvie, who was a confident man, 'there's been a thorough search of the area and there's no trace of any hair clippings.'

'Barber in town?' asked Crow.

'Luke McGowan,' said McLeod. 'All over the papers this morning giving his opinion on the haircuts. We questioned him yesterday just before the papers did. Says none of the victims had been to see him, so we have to go with that.'

'Unless he's the murderer,' said Crow.

'Nah,' said McLeod, shaking his head. 'Luke's been in the town since he was born. Everyone knows him. Never slit a throat in his life, not even unintentionally. Given his share of shit haircuts, I'll admit, but he's not been too bad since the doc started him on the valium shots.'

'They allowed to do that?' said Crow.

'For day to day stuff, aye,' answered McLeod. 'Not if they're in competition.'

Crow nodded, deciding to reserve judgement on Luke McGowan. He knew well not to write anyone out of an investigation, and it was ever the way of Federal agents to turn up in small towns throughout the States and be told who could and who couldn't have committed any given crime; just as it was equally the way for them to prove local law enforcement wrong. The case of Fingers Spaghetti and the murder of Little Boy Fettucini in the town of Plattsburgh in upstate New York, using only one slice of cherry pie, had been enough to prove that hypothesis. That they were now in Scotland instead of America, did not mean things were going to be any different.

'He's got an assistant, of course,' said McLeod,

continuing, 'but Igor's never hurt anyone.'

Crow looked up, a curious smile coming to his lips.

'Igor?' he said. 'He's got an assistant called Igor? You're shitting me, right?'

'He's always there if you want to go and talk to him,' said McLeod, shrugging. Garvie and McIntosh smiled. 'Not that he says much,' he added.

Fine, thought Crow, that would do it. He could speak to McGowan and his able assistant himself.

He hooked the strip of yellow and black tape above his head and walked into the crime scene to study the ground which had been well trodden beneath the trees. Cameron approached them, having read the full story of the stone circle, and having already made the decision that it was unrelated to the investigation.

'Hi,' she said to Garvie and McIntosh. 'Lara Cameron. My family left Scotland in 1643.'

3
Arf

Barney stood outside the barber shop looking up at the sign. *McGowan & Son, Hair Emporium.* The usual tired red and white pole outside the door, the usual paint slowly peeling off the window frame, the window in need of cleaning, cobwebs in the corner and dust on the sill inside. How did these people expect to attract customers with presentation like this?

He breathed deeply, his mind wandering. For two months now the newspapers had been running the same photograph of him, a photo which must have been given to them by someone at the old shop. Taken eleven years previously when he'd had a ridiculous 70's perm and had been toying with a moustache, so that he'd looked for all the world like some sort of major porn star. Barney the Bonker; Tonguetastic Thommo; Banging Barn, the Bare Bum Boogie Man; or Mr Sausage. It'd taken him less than a week to realise how much of an idiot he'd looked, and he'd quickly switched to a more subdued, if equally inappropriate, Tom Cruise. However, the photograph had been taken, the damage done. And he'd always been embarrassed by it, until now when the world thought he looked like this idiot with curly hair, when in fact he was just a guy.

Still, he thought, it could happen that someone would get hold of a more recent picture, it would get splashed everywhere, and his detection would be inevitable. It was time to equalise before they scored, and get a new look; some style or colour he'd never had before, so that there'd be no photographic evidence to follow him around.

He pushed open the door to the shop and walked in. There was a man sitting, reading the latest bestseller—*Women Read 'Men Are From Mars, Woman Are From Venus', Men Read The Sports Pages*—slouched back in one of the chairs. Another shorter, younger man, was stooped over a brush so that the curve of the hunch on his back was exaggerated even more.

With the opening of the door, the hunchback glanced round quickly, then resumed his sweeping. The other man jumped up and put the book down, turning in a flash from slouching, disinterested slob, to smooth-talking barber-type bloke, ready with a cape and a smile.

'Haircut?' said Barney, immediately depressed by his surroundings. Standard shop lay out, only two chairs, one of which was obviously permanently vacant. A general dingy feel to the place, the lighting low, and he immediately assumed that it was in order to cover up the more startling of the barber's inadequate cuts.

Along one wall was a selection of Hollywood photographs, with all the usual suspects. Brad Pitt, Johnny Depp, George Clooney, Pierce Brosnan, Russell Crowe, Martin Clunes. None of the photographs were the usual head shots of the barbershop, however. They were all casual photographs, the guys smiling and relaxing, as if they were all friends of McGowan and the pictures had been taken while they were hanging out together, sinking a few beers.

'Certainly, sir,' said Luke McGowan, who'd had a slow

33

day, since the news of the freshly shorn murder victims had been in the papers.

Barney took off his jacket, hung it on a peg which looked as if it was not long for the wall, and slid cautiously into the chair. On the other side of the hirsutological fence, he was feeling the same things as his old customers had been used to. He caught Igor looking at him and nodded uncomfortably.

'Hi,' said Barney, and Igor sort of grunted in reply, so that it sounded like he said *arf*.

'Here we go, again, eh?' said McGowan not wanting Barney to dwell in attempted conversation with his less than loquacious assistant.

Barney caught his eye quickly in the mirror. Assumed he was talking about the murders.

'The weather, I mean,' said McGowan, sensing Barney's confusion. 'Nightmare. What d'you make of that, eh?'

'Aye,' said Barney, having a sudden insight into how all the poor sods whose hair he had put to the sword over the years, while he droned on about the weather, must have felt. Not quite a moment of epiphany, because moments of epiphany are made of more than that, but close to it.

McGowan studied his scissors, while he checked out Barney's hair.

'What'll it be?' he decided to ask, because he had a strange feeling that Barney might be a man who'd expect more than the straightforward.

'You got any dye?' asked Barney, his mind already made up.

McGowan shrugged. Had had some in a cupboard for close on twenty years—men didn't get their hair dyed much in Strathpeffer—and he assumed it'd be all right.

'What colour you looking for?' asked McGowan.

'A kind of reddy brown would do it,' said Barney, thinking that might not be too far away from his eyebrows and beard. 'A number one at the sides, number three on top,' he added.

Different enough from the way he was, but not too radical as to draw attention to himself.

'Should be no problem,' said McGowan. 'Igor, get the dye from the cupboard, will you?'

'Arf,' grunted Igor, and he laid the broom against the wall and shuffled off to the store room out back.

'You want me to do the cut first?' asked McGowan.

A car drove past outside, it's silencer busted, roaring noisily through the cold and dark of late afternoon. Barney caught McGowan's eye in the mirror, thinking that even someone who'd never been to a barber in their life wouldn't ask that question.

'Aye,' said Barney, 'cut first, then dye.'

'Excellent,' said McGowan, and he downed his scissors, lifted the electric razor, blew across the top of it—spitting on it at the same time—and studied Barney's head again.

'There's something bugging me,' said McGowan, adopting a chatty, conversational tone, and Barney thought, here we go. 'Something niggling at the back of my mind. A clawing thought, scraping away at my subconscious, a whore to my spirit, digging like the eager talons of suspicion at the scales of my curiosity, piercing the very skin of my self-assurance, a malignant tumour of discontent, scratching with the astringent unguis of angst at the desert of my aplomb. You know what I mean?'

'Totally,' said Barney.

'I can never work out,' said McGowan, 'what it is that's going on with cows.'

Barney half smiled, but really, there was no need for what was about to happen. McGowan could just shut up and get on with the cut. But no, he was a barber, therefore he would feel duty-bound to spout endless amounts of total tripe. It was part of the whole ethos, after all. What makes a barber a barber, and not just a guy with a pair of scissors.

'Cows?' said Barney, playing the game.

'Aye,' said McGowan, still surveying the scene in front of him, still wondering where to start. 'You get fields and fields of cows, right. Thousands of them all over the country. But where are all the bulls? You don't get fields of them, do you? You just get the odd bull here and there, stuck away in a field, like the embarrassing family member you don't want anyone to know about.'

He stopped, waiting for Barney to express interest, and when none was forthcoming, he continued anyway.

'So what's the score? Are there really eight million cows born to every bull? Is there some lost Land of the Bulls somewhere, hidden behind a secret doorway? Indiana Jones and the Land of the Bulls, that'd be a great movie, eh?'

'Aye,' said Barney without much enthusiasm.

'Or do they have a bovine Slaughter of the Innocents every week, when they round up all the male cattle and strike them down? It's fascinating, don't you think?'

'Aye,' said Barney, wishing that he'd asked for a 'nothing off the top, nothing off the sides and back', and could already have left.

Igor shuffled back into the room and placed an old bottle of hair dye, approximately the colour which Barney had requested, on the counter beside the inevitable sink.

'Thanks,' said McGowan.

'Arf,' grunted Igor.

Barney looked at the bottle and wondered whether to register a decision to change his mind about the dyeing business. Being British though, he never said anything.

'The thing I find really odd,' said McGowan, setting the razor going and upping the volume of his voice by an unnecessary margin, 'is when you see two cows humping,

36

because you do get that sometimes. I mean, do you get male cows? Or is it lesbian cow action? And if they are lesbian cows, what's the point of them humping like that?'

'Maybe,' said Barney, giving into the inevitable and joining the conversation, 'the farmer fits a prosthetic penis to the dominant one.'

Igor, once more bent over his brush, gave Barney a swift glance. McGowan nodded, as he careered wildly with the razor around the back of Barney's head, shearing off great galumphing clumps of hair in an entirely random manner.

'Aye,' he said, 'because there are going to be cows who prefer to dish it out than take it. The whole cow thing fascinates me. It's like a microcosm of human existence in every field.'

Just a couple of minutes and already the man was in overdrive. Talking beautiful bollocks, cutting a swathe through interesting conversation, turning the mundane into the criminally dull. Barney stared into the mirror, and recognised his past.

'Did you know that in Texas they give cows udder lifts and odour implants?' said McGowan.

Forty-five minutes later, Barney Thomson walked free from *McGowan & Son, Hair Emporium*, adorned with a very stiff short back and sides, hair a slightly different colour, and aware as never before of the agonies through which he had put his customers in the olden days.

4

There Came A Knock
At The Door,
And It Was Death

"Death never takes the wise man by surprise;
he is always ready to go.
The fool, on the other hand,
is liable to get a sharp spike up the bottom."
Jean de la Fontaine (1621-95)

The person who had killed the four students from West
Warwick, Rhode Island, was not by nature a psychopathic,
serial-killing, skin-ripping-off, psychotically deranged,
sociopathic, fifteen-cards-short-of-the-deck, suck-it-and-see,
blood-for-the-sake-of-blood kind of soul. With the exception
of the murder of a couple of Jehovah's, which the Judge had
described as 'no more than anyone else would have done
under the circumstances', life had been a laid back affair. As
a young boy he had been meek and mild, and his personality
had never really changed. However, the American students
had stumbled across a little secret. As it happened, the truth
was already out there, but that didn't mean it should go any
further than it already had. The students had been looking
to cause trouble, and so they had had to die.

Trouble was, however, that the bittersweet tang of blood

had now been tasted, and the thought had occurred that there was no need to let this particular sleeping dog lie. There were plenty more opportunities in the town to sate this new desire. Maybe none of them deserved to die, as such, but what the Hell, puttered playfully away in the killer's head that night, walking out into the bitter cold of a January evening. Death is as Death does, as they used to say in the Middle Ages.

And so, at 2215hrs, there came a knocking at the door of the Reverend Benjamin Wilson, a vicious old bugger who had ministered to ever dwindling numbers of these people for some thirty years or so.

Wilson looked at the digital clock—a gift from God—which hummed quietly away on his bedside table, and shook his head. He removed his reading glasses and laid down his copy of that month's *Big Breasted Lesbian Grannies*.

'For God's sake,' he muttered quietly to himself, cursing the fact that Mrs Wilson was no longer here to answer the late night calls for him; Mrs Wilson having absconded with a party of passing Dutch motorcycle tourists.

Draping his M&S dressing gown around his vigorously blue and white striped pyjamas, he clumped down the stairs, along the corridor—the floorboards of the old manse creaking noisily as ever—and up to the front door. The insistent rapping came again, just as he pulled the door open.

'All right,' said the Rev Wilson tetchily. 'Oh, it's you,' he said with, to be frank, no less irritation, when he saw who was without.

'Reverend,' said his killer-to-be. 'I was wondering if you had a minute?'

'It's after ten o'clock,' said the vicar, trying hard not to let the irritation enter his voice. Despite the fact that it was stamped on his face like he'd been trodden on by one of those wrestling guys from WWF. Or is it WWC. Or WFW. Or

WANK. (Not that you'd say that to their face.)

'I know, Reverend,' said the visitor, voice sounding fairly sincere, it has to be said, 'I just, I mean, I really need, you know, something's happened, and I really need to talk to someone.'

The vicar stared at his guest. The visitor returned the stare, imploringly.

'Please, Reverend, I don't know where else to turn.'

The Reverend Wilson allowed his face to break out into a concerned smile. His issue of *Big Breasted Lesbian Grannies* had arrived fresh from Florida that morning, but it could wait. And besides, if he kicked this person out by the backside, as he was disposed to do, it might get back to the church elders, and then he'd have Wee Aggie 4/12, as he liked to call her —because she seemed to be menstruating four weeks a month, twelve months of the year—round here like a horde of Mongol warriors on nandrolone.

'Very well,' he said, 'of course my door is always open.' But don't think for a minute that I'm offering you a cup of tea or cracking open the packet of Jaffa Cakes I bought at the supermarket this morning.

He held the door open and allowed the one who was about to take his life, to walk unhindered into his home. Almost as if Death himself had arrived, black cape drawn Obi Wan-style down over his head, and had been invited in for a late night snifter.

They sat down on sofas on opposite sides of the coffee table, the Reverend Wilson wincing slightly at the amount of dust which had accumulated in the three and half years since Mrs Wilson had departed. (He'd told everyone in the village that she'd died, paid MacDuff the Undertaker and McLeod the policeman to keep schtoom, and had conducted a very moving funeral service.)

'What seems to be the trouble?' said Wilson, clasping

40

his hands on his thighs, and attempting to convey concern. Really he couldn't have cared less if this person—or anyone else on the planet, for that matter—got knocked down by a bus.

The killer swallowed and stared at the floor. Might as well string it out a little bit longer; piss the old man off and distract him from reading that sleazy porn that everyone says he busies himself with at night. Wilson waited patiently, his thoughts drifting back to Hilda Grace Rubenstein, 69, from Cedar Ridge and Greta-Mae Koslovsky, 71, from Big Falls.

'It's those four tourists,' said the killer. 'I'm really worried.'

Wilson looked up, and thought for a second he could detect genuine fear in the eyes of this errant parishioner, who had never attended one of his services.

'There's no need to worry,' said Wilson, leaning forward, curiosity mingling with an almost unfeigned concern. 'It was an isolated case. That it happened in Blackmuir Wood meant nothing. Don't worry for a second that this tragedy will be visited upon any of the residents of the town.'

The killer also leant forward, nodding slowly, wiping a finger beneath the left eye, as if taking away a tear. Wilson's curiosity was actually dragging him into this thing. He hadn't thought that anyone would be that bothered about it, apart from the possible adverse effects on tourism. Even then, for everyone frightened off, there's a goon waiting in line to come and check out the Town of Death.

'The mind of the perfect man is a mirror,' said the vicar, strangely. 'It does not lean forward or backward in its response to things. It responds to things but conceals nothing of its own. Therefore it is able to deal with things without injury to its reality.'

The killer stared at the vicar. As a young lad his mother had dragged him incessantly along to church, at least once a

41

week, sometimes twice or more. And it had fostered within him a hearty disrespect for all these men of God.

'Look, Bishop,' the killer said, waving away Wilson's protestations about the bishop thing, 'you might think you impress people by quoting Chuang Tzu, but to be perfectly honest with you, Chinese philosophy gets up my arse, you know what I'm saying?'

'Very well,' said Wilson, a little irritated. The quote had been completely inappropriate, but he generally found it useful in awkward conversational moments when his flock were looking for guidance, to quote any old crap that they'd assume came from the Bible. He'd quote the Bible itself, but he hadn't read it in over fifty years and couldn't really remember much of it. There were a couple of bits about Jesus that rang a bell, and he was fairly confident about the story of Moses up to the point where he gets stuck in the basket, but after that he was hopeless. 'What would you like me to do for you?'

'No, no,' said the killer, smiling broadly now, shaking his head again. 'You've got me wrong, your worshipfulness. I don't need your help. I'm here to help you.'

Wilson sat back, straightened his shoulders, and looked witheringly across the table. This was not someone who could help him in any way, and if he was about to be asked the question which he presumed he was, his late night guest could get the Hell out of Sodom and leave him in peace.

'I can't begin to imagine what that might be,' said Wilson.

'That is because you have so little imagination,' said the killer, who inched forward, then added, 'To that high Capital, where kingly Death keeps his pale court in beauty and decay, he came!' quoting the poet Shelley and getting a little overexcited as the words flowed.

'What?' said the bish.

'You're about to die, old man,' said the visitor.

The Reverend Wilson was still confused. So, in order to swiftly bring this general air of verbal chaos to a conclusion, the killer of the four American tourists rose swiftly, produced a pair of hairdressing scissors—a classic set of Buckmaster Texans, circa 1947—raised them dramatically aloft in a staged movement, paused briefly to enjoy the look of terror that suddenly manifested itself on the old man of God's face, then leapt at him across the coffee table, a massive powerful leap, so that when the scissors thumped into the vicar's face, they plunged through his eye socket and penetrated deeply into the back of his head.

A rather strange little cry was ejaculated from the pit of his throat, and it sounded like *'ye were as a firebrand plucked out of the burning'*, just going to show that all the Bible stuff that he thought he'd forgotten, had actually just lain dormant in his subconscious, waiting for his moment of death. Didn't mean he was going to get into Heaven though.

The killer took another moment, as the end of the vicar's strange words dribbled from his twitching bottom lip, looked curiously at the old man, engaging the eye that wasn't beholden to a pair of scissors, then, with another well practised and vicious movement, withdrew the implement of murder, and immediately thrust it into the bish's chest. Another noise escaped, this time a scarcely audible grunt, as the air was squeezed from his lungs.

The killer straightened up, breaths coming quickly with the shock of carrying out the execution, and, just as had happened with the execution of the four tourists, hands shaking and heart thumping lustily. For after years of searching, a true vocation had been found.

The killer looked around the room, and it did not take long to find the perfect canvas for the face of death, drawn in blood.

5

Kierkegaard Ate My Hamster

"What is a good hair cut? Nothing but the paint
on the face of Existence; the least touch
of truth rubs it off, and then we see what a
hollow-cheeked harlot we have got hold of."
Lord Byron (1788-1824)

As late night drifted into the early hours of the morning,
there was a strange collective in the bar of the Highland
Inn, some time after the Reverend Wilson was despatched
from his grumbling miserable misery of miseries to an even
more miserable eternal misery of miseries. There were eight
people in the bar, as well as Bobby the Barman, who was
looking forward to a late night snack, the exact nature of
which you really, really don't want to know about.

There was Legal Attaché Cameron of the Federal
Bureau of Investigation, (Crow having disappeared for the
evening on some sidetrack, the nature of which he had kept
from his assistant). Legendary serial killer Barney Thomson.
Theodore Wolf, marketing consultant, who was stopping over
in Strathpeffer for a few days while he sorted out the
Highlands in a manner of differing ways. Alec McGowan,
barber, and his beauteous assistant Igor. Detective Sergeant
McLeod of the Northern Constabulary. And finally, Earl
Strathcaln, a curious little man who owned large areas of

land north of Inverness, a man who had dabbled in politics until a scandal involving another man's bottom had been the death of it, and who now spent his days shooting whatever local wildlife happened to be in season, and being pleasured by the Thai woman he had bought through a catalogue agency three years previously, Soo Yin, who was also submissively in attendance.

Barney was keen on having an evening alone. Time to mull over his troubles and consider his next step, as his fiscal situation really demanded that he move on the next day, there being no work that he could reasonably consider in the area. However, he had ended up being sucked into a group involving Alec McGowan, Igor, Strathcaln and his missus. Cameron was sitting with McLeod discussing various serial killers she'd come across in her time; while McLeod told unspeakable tales of illegal late night salmon fishing and internecine strife in Contin. Theodore Wolf sat alone at the bar, watching over the others and occasionally trading the verbal equivalent of the contents of a septic tank with Bobby the Barman.

And in amongst this weird collective, the quintuple murderer sat and chatted, casual and relaxed like any other, hands washed of the blood of the Reverend Wilson, the racing heart that had so pumped with the thrusting of the knife, now settled to a steady beat.

'It's the whole pleasure-pain thing,' the barber McGowan was saying, coming towards the end of a fifteen hour diatribe on the equal and opposite *nature of things*. Barney was bored.

'You mean the principles of felicific calculus,' said Earl Strathcaln, 'where you're talking the dimensions of intensity, duration, certainty, propinquity, purity, fecundity and extent.'

'Aye,' said McGowan, not really having a clue what Strathcaln was talking about, and a little put out at having the thrust of the conversation stolen from him.

'The thing is,' continued Strathcaln, 'that felicific calculus depends on the concept that a set quantum purport of potency is equivalent to a quantum purport of existence, which rests on a perfidious analogy with spatial measurement, thereby negating the whole utilitarian ethical theory nonsense.'

The others stared at him, it being the first time he'd spoken in some ten minutes. Even Barney had been more erudite.

'Oh,' said McGowan, his gas at a peep.

'Arf,' growled Igor.

'Did any of what you just said make any sense, whatsoever?' said Barney, attuned as usual to the bullshitter's wavelength.

Strathcaln gave Barney a snooty look, as Legal Attaché Cameron passed by the table on her way to the bar. Strathcaln thought of many things to say in reply to Barney, but decided the man with badly dyed orange-brown hair wasn't worth the effort.

Cameron stood at the bar, her elbows resting on the counter.

'Hi,' she said, as Bobby the Barman approached.

'What can I get you?' asked Bobby, with that little extra enthusiasm in his voice which he reserved for attractive women.

'I'm Lara Cameron,' she said, 'my family left Scotland in 1643.'

'I know,' said Bobby the Barman, 'you introduced yourself earlier. Three or four times, as a matter of fact.'

'Oh,' said Cameron. 'Did I say I've got a cousin in Falkirk?'

'Yeah,' said Bobby the Barman, 'And that you'd seen Braveheart eighteen times.'

'Great movie,' she said.

'What'll it be?' asked Bobby the Barman.

'Neat whisky for the sergeant, and I'll have a Bud.'

'No problemo,' said Bobby the Barman, quickly going about his business.

A few yards away along the bar, Theodore Wolf leant forward.

'To work a wonder, God would have her shown, at once, a bud, and yet a rose full-blown,' he said.

Cameron stared at him. She'd been in the country long enough to know that a lot of the inhabitants were even stranger than she was herself.

'What?' she asked.

'You mentioned bud,' said Wolf, moving slowly along the bar.

'And?' said Cameron.

'Robbert Herrick, seventeenth century poet,' said Wolf.

'I don't think they had Budweiser in those days, friend,' said Cameron.

Wolf smiled.

'I tried to think of a quote involving Budweiser, but the only one I could come up with was Bud-weis-er,' he said, croaking out the last word. 'Bud-weis-er,' he croaked again, smiling.

Cameron also smiled. She was a cheerful sort, really, but she could spot a marketing man a mile off—although, who can't—and she had no time for them. Not since she'd bought a Metz thinking it was going to have some sort of kick to it.

'How about, "piss off, fella, or I'll stick a bottle of Budweiser up your ass?"' she said

Wolf smiled. Being a marketing man, he wasn't to be daunted.

'That Florence Nightingale, was it?' he said.

Bobby the Barman put the drinks on the bar. Cameron

shook her head, decided she wasn't going to engage Wolf any further, lifted the drinks and turned back towards McLeod. Wolf and Bobby the Barman watched her go, the movement of her legs and buttocks emphasised by her clinging black skirt.

'What d'you make of that?' said Wolf.

'Apart from the family leaving Scotland thing,' said Bobby the Barman, 'which, to be frank, is getting on my tits, she's a bit of all right. Great feet.'

'Lovely,' said Wolf, supping from the dregs of his pint of lager, 'me too. Think I might make a serious attempt at it if I can get her away from the policeman.'

'Good luck,' said Bobby the Barman, thinking he had more chance himself, especially now with his great complexion 'n all.

And they both continued to stare at her as she sat back down beside McLeod. Passing the other table, she had briefly caught Barney's eye, there had been the slightest of acknowledgements between the two of them, and then Barney had looked away first, perturbed almost at being eyed up by a woman.

And as she began to regale McLeod with further details on the case of Snickers McGhee and how he'd used a chocolate bar as the instrument of murder in more than three hundred killings, Barney had a question thrown directly at him, which was even more disconcerting than catching the eye of an attractive woman.

'So, to which camp do you belong?' asked the barber McGowan of Barney. 'Hegel or Kierkegaard?'

Barney stared briefly at McGowan. There was a time when he would've risen to the discussion, even leapt at it like a lemur dancing between the dinosaurs—because lemurs and dinosaurs were big together, you know—but now he had no spirit for the discussion, and the inevitable argument. Not so long ago he would've sat in the pub with his mate Bill Taylor, hunched over a pint of lager and a game of dominoes, discussing the merits of Kierkegaard, until they were punted out into the early hours of the morning, stinking of booze and fags. But now the pith of his id had been crushed like dried up dog faeces squished beneath the foot of a twenty-eight stone woman, eating another fish supper and wearing size fifteen boots.

'Kierkegaard was a wank,' he said solemnly, and looked at the small clock behind the bar. Almost twelve-thirty. He'd sat in this company long enough.

'Humph,' said McGowan, staring at his beer. As it happened he also considered Kierkegaard to be a bit of a wank, but then he usually liked to arrive at that conclusion after several hours of considered argument.

'Arf,' said Igor. Had he been able to say something other than *arf*, he would have articulated the opinion that Kierkegaard had been right to proclaim the perspicuity of God and man, and the unaccountability of the correlation between the two. He would also have pointed out that, as Heidegger stated, man is an evanescent being, aware, through the opalescence of his animus, of the certitude of his own death, and therefore, the only way to get up in the morning and face your breakfast cereal with added vitamins and low fat milk, is in full cognisance of *le néant*, until you've worked the whole thing out for yourself. Still, ever the mute hunchback's place to be considered an idiot.

Barney drained his glass, looked around the table—Strathcaln had no opinion on Kierkegaard, other than to wonder if he was bloke who won the men's downhill at the Lake Placid Olympics in 1984; Soo Yin had studied all the great Danish philosophers, Kierkegaard, Schmeichel, Maesrk Line, Holsten Pils, but knew better than to open her mouth in public—nodded at the assembled company, and slowly rose from his seat.

As he stood up, he once again caught the eye of Lara Cameron, currently side-tracked into a discussion on whether Marino would've won a Superbowl ring had he been with anyone but the Dolphins. They stared at each other for a few seconds, and then once again it was Barney who broke eye contact, and quickly turned and walked away through the bar, into the reception area, under the dead stag, and on up the stairs. And he wondered with every step, why it was that he was drawn to this woman who would surely suspect him of the murder of the four tourists, if she were to find out his true identity.

f

Early morning in Strathpeffer, still bitterly cold and consumed by darkness. 0430hrs, the town, for the most part, still sleeping an untroubled sleep. Not until the following afternoon would the brutalised body of the Reverend Wilson be discovered.

Barney Thomson slept a very troubled sleep, because that's what he did these days. This night he dreamed a strange thing involving an enormous spider, three tonnes of West African-style cement, a bottle of Miller Lite and a prostitute called Epiphany with fifty-six inch hips and no breasts, who continually announced, 'Hi, I'm Epiphany, my family left Scotland in a boat.' And so he tossed and turned, his eyes roaming continuously, pushing against the lids, his mouth open, his breath uneven.

At this time Damien Crow finally returned to the hotel, let himself in, passed beneath the dead stag—who was a little put out at being awoken in the middle of the night—and walked up to his room. Lara Cameron, who was wide awake, staring at the ceiling, her room illuminated by the light from the streets, heard him enter his room next door. She looked at the clock, made a mental note of the time, then turned over and closed her eyes.

Luke McGowan was fast asleep. Igor slept in the room next to his, in the small flat above the shop. He lay awake, as usual—Igor never slept—staring at the large map of the world above his bed. And he imagined all the places he was going to go, when he was able to leave Strathpeffer, and of all the strange and exotic countries in the world where people would accept him for who he was, rather than for the hump on his back, and for the fact that no matter what he tried to say in life, it always only ever came out as *arf*.

Theodore Wolf slept the sleep of the marketing consultant. Easy and confident, in the knowledge that tomorrow would bring even more money than today. Bastard.

Strathcaln lay on his side, back turned to Soo Yin, trying to sleep. His mind was troubled, however, and sleep would not come to ease him. Soo Yin had long since given in to her subconscious, and was breathing heavily beside him. A change from the early days of the marriage, when she had lain awake at night, feeling the cold, and missing her friends and the bustle and excitement of Bangkok.

Detective Sergeant McLeod dreamt about the feet of Lara Cameron, whose family had left Scotland in 1643.

Bobby the Barman slept deeply, and dreamt of nothing.

6

Sausages

The morning dawned cold and frosty, the sky unusually blue. The town had come to life during the hours of darkness, as is the way of the Highlands during the winter, what with it not getting light until well into the morning.

Barney sat alone at breakfast, head down in a corner, thinking. He was hoping that Theodore Wolf would not feel obliged to join him. Hoping and dreading at the same time the possibility of Lara Cameron sitting next to him. Not to know that Cameron and Crow were already up and out for the day, a crucial part of the investigation to be undertaken.

He tucked into the full Highland breakfast, for the second morning in a row. Eggs, bacon, haggis, mushrooms, fried bread, tomatoes and three hundred and fourteen different types of sausage. More toast than you could shake a stick at and enough tea to drown a bull's bollocks, as they say in these parts.

Towards the end of his marathon face-cramming-fest, his plate cleared of all the essential coronary-inducing ingredients and only twenty-seven slices of toast still to be disposed of, he was considering the possibility of doing a grand dine and dash, leaving the hotel by a back door, not paying for any of it and heading onto the next hotel down the road. If he could spend weeks and months on the run for murder, how difficult could it be to spend his life moving from hotel to hotel without ever paying the bill?

Anyway, he would never be able to tell what it was that brought a new thought into his head; maybe the colour of the marmalade, maybe the consistency of the tea, maybe the music that drifted down from the PA system, maybe the waitress who flirted by asking if he'd like some more toast, but something suddenly struck him about the night before, a bizarre little moment of epiphany—this was a real moment of epiphany among so many fakes—about one of his eight confederates in the bar, something that seemed obvious now that it was in his head, but which hadn't been obvious the previous evening.

And once the thought was there it wouldn't go away, and suddenly he'd eaten enough. The toast tasted dry, the marmalade bitter. He took one last slurp of tea and laid the white cup down in its saucer. He looked around the small restaurant. Nothing had changed; no one else there had had the same thought as he. On the other side of the room, Theodore Wolf was eating his fifteenth kipper, and was himself looking around the assembled company, wondering how many people he could persuade to buy the new chocolate covered meatballs for which he'd won the contract.

Barney avoided his eye and looked down at the table. His sudden insight did not necessarily mean anything in itself, did not necessarily point to the perpetrator of the murders. However, it might be worth following up. So, he could point the authorities in the direction of his suspicions, he could do a bit of investigating himself, or he could turn his back and walk away, because this had nothing whatsoever to do with him; despite what the raft of that morning's newspaper headlines suggested. *The London Times*—Thomson Continues Cull of Planet; *The Sun*—Barber Surgeon Eats Testicles of Live Goat; *The New York Times*—No Truth in Thomson Marriage Rumours, Claims Ex-Dallas Star; *The Washington Post*—Demon Barber In Bizarre Late Night West Wing Visits; *The Daily Mirror*—Barcelona Sign Ace Crimper For £150M; *Astronaut Weekly*—Thomson In Shock NASA 'Serial Killer In Space' Tests; *The National Enquirer*—Thomson To Be Part Of Pammy Anderson's New Breasts; *The Ross-shire Journal*—Nightmare For Mrs McKay As Chicken Not Defrosted In Time For Dinner.

Barney stood up and began to walk through the restaurant. In the past he might have been filling himself with steely determination, buckling down to the task at hand, gathering up great handfuls of the spunk of resolve in order to wade into the issue with all guns blazing. Now, however, he couldn't even decide if he wanted to think about the issue, never mind ask it for a dance. And so he trudged out of the restaurant, through the bar, took the usual walk under the miserable looking, dear-departed stag, and pounded the stairway beat back up to his room.

It had not taken Legal Attaché Crow long to come to the same conclusion as Barney Thomson. It had only been a passing thing, a chance encounter during the first day of their investigation, but it had been enough to make him ask the question. And while anyone of immediate interest to him sat in the bar the previous evening, he had let himself into three homes in the Strathpeffer area. He had found nothing conclusive to the murder investigation, although he had confirmed the suspicion that both he and Barney had come to.

He found a few interesting things in the flat above the barber shop; Detective Sergeant McLeod's house gave up no end of secrets; and Strathcaln's house revealed everything that he thought it would.

Now they were on their way down to Edinburgh, a task that did not require both of them. But Crow thought that he had all the time in the world, not realising that the Reverend Wilson had already been murdered, and that the slaughter would continue if unchecked.

'You going to tell me where we're going?' said Cameron, looking up from another story in the local rag: *Rosemarkie Lads In Football Stramash*.

'Edinburgh,' said Crow, who had hauled her out of bed, thrust a cup of coffee in her face, tossed her into the shower, and waited for her in the car.

They were already nearly at Perth, having been sat on the A9 for a little under an hour and a half. They had been stopped by an unmarked police car while doing 130mph through the Drumochter pass; Crow had flashed his FBI credentials and Police Constable Storie had told him 'not to be so bloody stupid' and booked him anyway. That aside, things had been fairly uneventful. Cameron had waited for Crow to tell her what they were doing, and had finally cracked when no explanation was forthcoming.

'It's about twenty miles from Falkirk, before you ask,' he added.

'What's in Edinburgh?' she asked, ignoring the Falkirk remark.

'Lots of things,' said Crow.

'You going to tell me any of them?' she asked, not in the least irritated. She was well used to Crow, the fact that he pretty much kept everything in life to himself, and also safe in the knowledge that when she really needed to know something, he'd tell her.

'Nope,' said Crow. 'Not unless you can work some of it out for yourself.'

Cameron smiled.

'You realise everyone else in the Bureau thinks you're a pain in the ass?'

Crow smiled as he began an horrendously extravagant overtaking manoeuvre past a slow moving old man in a slow moving old car.

'Yeah,' he said, 'that's why they sent me to London. What's your excuse? They want you to be closer to your ancestors?'

She shook her head and stared out of the window at the cold fields and rolling hills that line the road as you approach Perth. She decided to play the game, and tried to think of who and what they had seen since their arrival in the Highlands. It had been a little under a day, and so far it seemed to her that they had skirted around the investigation with no real inroads made, no salient—as Deputy Assistant Director Helmar back in Washington was fond of saying—to exploit.

The crime scene had yielded little. The local SOCO's had already sent several items back to a laboratory for investigation, and whoever had done the work had been thorough. Crow had gone in with his usual lack of respect for anyone else's investigative methods, presuming that he would unearth several items that the others had been unable to find. This time, however, the cupboard had been bare.

They had set about tracing everyone that the four students had been in contact with since their arrival in the area. The victims had stayed at the Strathpeffer youth hostel, but the police had already been over it, and all the others staying there—which wasn't too many given the time of year—and discovered everything that was there to be found.

It wasn't much. The American students had been in the

country for less than two days, having arrived in the Highlands by train from London. They had hitchhiked from Inverness to Strathpeffer, one of them having read about it in a book, and having decided it was a good place to start a brief walking tour of the area. They had spent their first night in the bar of the Highland Inn, which was where they first came across their murderer. They talked to anyone who was interested; one of them got into a lengthy discussion with Bobby the Barman on waste products; another discussed land reform and the proliferation of farm animals suffering psychological difficulties related to lack of parental affection with Strathcaln and his missus, not that Soo Yin Strathcaln had had much to say on the matter; one of them spent nearly an hour discussing the marketing of Nike with Theodore Wolf; the same guy had also chatted long into the evening with Igor about the Hertzsprung-Russell diagram and the evolution of stars from blue-bright to red-dim, although the conversation was a little one way; and in general they mixed and chatted and made moves on anything that was female. A typical 'guys on a world tour with not much money to spend' type of evening. More talk than drink, and those who were present had very little to say about the four students, other than that they had seemed very personable and that they'd all been in need of a good stiff haircut.

After leaving the hostel at nine-thirty the following morning, a foggy day when they were advised to stay off the hills and confine themselves to walking in the woods which encircled the town, they were never seen again. Or at least, not so that anyone was saying.

Cameron slowly emerged from her ruminations on the investigation and looked at Crow. They were now past Perth and heading towards Edinburgh on the M90. The sun that had followed them all the way so far was beginning to be covered by thin cloud, the little warmth that it was bringing to the day being slowly dissipated.

'Don't get it,' she said.

Crow nodded but didn't say anything.

'You going to tell me?' she asked.

'Nah,' he said, without turning to look at her. 'Watch and learn.'

Cameron breathed deeply and closed her eyes. She was tired, and maybe that was why she couldn't think as clearly as she'd like. Or maybe it was just because Crow was being totally obscure and there was no way she was going to be able to work it out.

'You know all those folk in the Bureau who think you're a pain in the ass?' she said. 'They're right.'

Crow smiled, moved into the outside lane, cutting up a sales rep in that month's 406, and accelerated smoothly up to and on past the hundred mark.

7

Mike Yarwood

"Go, teach Eternal Wisdom how to rule -
Then drop into thyself, and be a fool!
I often act foolish because I can,
Just like Bugs Bunny and Desperate Dan."
                              Alexander Pope (1688-1744)

A few hours later, and cold morning had already turned to
cold afternoon. Barney looked in the mirror. He was sitting
in the room which he was due to vacate some time in the
next hour or so—the housemaid had already been around
once and would be back soon, badgering to get the sheets
changed and the toilet paper recharged—studying his hair.

It was a competent job, nothing more than that.
Adequate. No imagination had been invested in the cut, and
little skill, but still, it was not in any way a shocker. It wasn't
the work of a complete ham-fisted balloon with a pair of
scissors, as he had first suspected he might receive when he
walked into McGowan & Son. So, although it was within
the wit of any barber to cut beneath their ability, the idea
that it might have been Luke McGowan who visited the
Heaven's Gate cuts on the four students, seemed unlikely. It
needn't necessarily be the case that the man who had cut the
students' hair was the same man who had committed the

murders, but it seemed likely. So, Barney was prepared to rule McGowan from the picture. Which left approximately five million other people in Scotland as suspects. Barney wasn't really cut out to be a detective.

He had still to make up his mind if he was going to follow the hunch that had come to him like an angel before the shepherds at breakfast. He had made up his mind about one thing, however. The brown dye that had been put in his hair, and had slowly turned orange, so that he looked like, well, an idiot, had to go. So, he had two choices. He either bought some dyeing agent from the local store and went about the business himself, or he went back to see Luke McGowan, and this time accepted no less than the best.

He should have done it himself, but something was dragging him back to that shop. Either a weird kind of cosmic thing, or more likely, just the fact that it was any old barber shop and he hankered for the old days of only a few months previously, when he would have spent eight hours of his life at the chair, every working day of the year. While suddenly being presented with freedom and no responsibility, the things that so many might crave in this complicated world, he was finding himself unnerved and alone, in need of comfort and a rock to cling to. The local barber shop was the only rock he could think of.

So he finally walked downstairs to check out of the hotel, paying the bill in cash, thereby leaving himself barely enough money to see him through the rest of the week. He had made the decision to head for Inverness, get a small job wherever he could, keep his head down, get a room and live an anonymous life until he could think of where he wanted to be in life.

He crossed the road and walked the few hundred yards to the barbershop, and this time he did not hesitate at the door. He intended getting his hair sorted, then he would walk out of Strathpeffer the way he had arrived, back down to the A835 and he would start walking the sixteen miles to Inverness. Maybe he would thumb a lift, and maybe he wouldn't bother.

He pushed the door open, and the usual suspects turned and looked at him as he entered. This time, however, there was a man in the chair, the ubiquitous Detective Sergeant McLeod. Barney hesitated when he saw him, but the best way to guarantee suspicion at this stage would've been for him to turn his back. So he did his best to continue smoothly into the shop and took his place on the small row of seats opposite the barber chairs.

There were general nods between the men, although Igor, who was sweeping God knows what at the rear of the shop, viewed Barney with the greatest suspicion, wondering if he had come to ask for the hair that he'd had cut the day before back. Well, thought Igor, you're not getting it.

'Arf,' he muttered under his breath.

'Oh, aye?' said Luke McGowan, looking at Barney in the mirror, having turned back to continue with McLeod's cut—a 15-Point Buckminsterfullerene, no less—'what's all this?'

Barney indicated his hair with his eyes.

'Turned out ugly,' he said. 'That dye you used was a bit past it, eh?'

McGowan stopped and turned to look at him properly. He grunted an acknowledgement that Barney did indeed look like an idiot, then he resumed McLeod's cut, his scissors clicking sweetly in the quiet of the shop.

'So,' McGowan began, having been interrupted by Barney's arrival, 'the thing about the Impressionists was that none of them could actually paint. Auguste Renoir, Camille Pissarro, Claude Monet, Michelle Platini, Kelly Le Brock, Joie De Vivre, Christopher Lambert, none of them. It was all faked.'

'That right?' said McLeod. 'Who painted all those pictures then?''

'That's the thing,' said McGowan, 'that none of these bum fluffs who pay millions for the paintings actually know.' And he stopped talking while he stuck his tongue between his teeth as he attempted a particularly delicate operation around the left ear. McLeod was waiting with curiosity, his eyes stuck on McGowan's protruding tongue. Barney listened with raised eyebrow, Igor swept slowly, wishing he could contradict.

'It was,' said McGowan, knowing he had his audience reeled in, 'a wee fella in Glasgow by the name of Archie Potts. That's why all they paintings look the same.'

'That right?' said McLeod.

'Oh, aye,' said McGowan. 'And he also wrote *Ride of the Valkyries*, *Wuthering Heights* and the script for *Carry On Up The Khyber*. Very talented bloke. Could make a cake with the best of them as well, so they said.'

McLeod nodded, thinking that you learn something new every day. Barney said nothing. Neither did Igor.

Meanwhile a woman was running along the street outside, approaching very quickly, her breath coming in great heaving pants—which, as a wee aside, also describes her underwear—frantically looking for the local law enforcement. *Have you seen McLeod?* she would ask of anyone she passed, and gradually she was taking the magical mystery tour in the direction of the barbershop.

And so, as Luke McGowan was on the point of talking even more complete and utter drivel, the likes of which Barney would've been proud had he done it himself, the door to the shop was flung open, and Margaret Hutchinson, she of the heaving pants, stood breathlessly in the doorway, hardly able to speak, panic on her face, and the slightest sign of sick on her beige coat.

'Margaret,' said McLeod, 'what's happened?'

'Sgt,' she said, gasping, 'it's the vicar.'

McLeod stood immediately, tearing the cape from around his neck—a bit of a Batman in reverse, sort of affair. His hair, sadly, was only half complete, but sometimes when you're in law enforcement you just have to accept that you're going to look like an idiot. That was why Superman was prepared to do the thing with his y-fronts on top of his leggings.

'What about him?' said McLeod.

'He's dead!' wailed Mrs Hutchinson. 'Murdered!' she ejaculated, at an even higher pitch.

'God!' said McLeod. 'Did you find the body?'

'Aye,' said the wailing woman, 'just now. I'm in shock. Shock!'

McLeod put his arms around her and hugged her tightly, bringing her head into his chest, and touching her hair.

'Don't worry, Margaret,' he said. 'Leave this to me.'

She tried to say something, but only another great sob came from the back of her throat. The other three men in the shop stood and watched this little drama, thinking, oh for goodness sake. It wasn't as if any of them hadn't seen their fair share of dead bodies.

'When did you discover the body?' asked McLeod.

'Just now!' she wailed. 'Just now! I went round with Benjamin's shopping.'

McLeod pulled her away from his chest so that he could look her in the eye.

'I know you're in shock,' said McLeod, 'but are you sure he was dead?'

'I don't know,' she blubbered. 'There was blood!'

'Did you establish time and cause of death?' asked McLeod. 'Was the murder weapon evident? Had there been a struggle? Do you think his killer left any DNA samples? What about fingerprints?'

She looked at him much as you would.

'Come on,' said Luke McGowan, grabbing his coat from the wall, 'the killer might still be there. Call it into Inverness, and let's get round there. Come on, Igor!'

'Arf,' said Igor.

'Right,' said McLeod. And in this moment of brief panic, when all that was required was a certain cool-headed rationale, an equanimity of spirit to mollify the situation, a serene tranquillity to ease the mind of the belaboured Mrs Hutchinson, mixed with a tranquil sang-froid, establishing control and putting the minds of the public at ease, Detective Sergeant McLeod was ably demonstrating why he was destined never to go any higher in law enforcement. He wasn't afraid of coming across the vicar's killer, not at all. It was just that he was absolutely crap in a crisis. 'Right,' he said again. 'You come with us,' he said to Barney, having no idea who he was, but thinking that collecting a group of able bodied men might be the job.

Barney thought of objecting, but strangely didn't. He just shrugged his shoulders, and said, 'All right.'

'Good,' said McLeod.

Luke McGowan charged from the shop, Igor following behind. Barney looked at Mrs Hutchinson, wondering what was going to become of her, but McLeod had a plan.

'Right, Margaret,' he said, 'you stay here and, eh, you know, cut anyone's hair if they come in.'

She looked mildly panicked at the suggestion—more at being left alone, than having to cut anyone's hair, because after all, she was one of over three thousand townsfolk who were more able hairdressers than McGowan—but before she could voice an objection, McLeod had pushed Barney out of the door in front of him, and was already charging off in the direction of his car to radio in the news of the vicar's death.

The door closed behind him, and Margaret Hutchinson stood in the quiet of the shop, surrounded by dirty walls and a sepulchral stillness that she could call her own. She turned round, her breaths still coming jerkily, and looked at the photos of the stars and their hair, and the two tatty old barber chairs, and the cuttings from the head of Detective Sergeant McLeod.

The door opened. Her heart leapt like a wounded bull into her mouth—she had actually had a wounded bull leap into her mouth on one occasion, and it'd been really painful—and she swivelled on a sixpence and looked at the door. A young man stood there, looking confident and cool, but not in the least serial killer-ish. She put her hand to her heart—which was back where it belonged—and tried to calm her breathing down enough to speak.

'Can I get a haircut?' said the man.

'I suppose,' said Margaret Hutchinson. 'What would you like?'

'Oh,' said the man, 'I was looking for a Zhang Chunqiao '76.'

Mrs Hutchinson breathed deeply and began to remove her coat. A glass of water and a few minutes chat before kicking off the cut, and she might be all right. The Zhang Chunqiao '76 was fairly straightforward.

'No problem,' she said. And the young fellow removed his coat and took his place in the chair by the mirror.

'So,' said Mrs Hutchinson, quickly taking on the necessary persona, 'you're a follower of Chinese politics? To be perfectly honest, I always thought that that Wang Hongwen was a bit of a knob.'

8

A Big, Big Finish

"The Thane of Fife had a wife:
where is she now?
The Thane of Mersey had a Jersey:
the stupid cow."
MacBeth (1606) act 4, sc. 3

Crow and Cameron had not been long in Edinburgh. They had found out what they needed to know, had stopped for a quick sandwich, and had sped back up the A9 at an average of somewhere approaching 140mph. He was booked twice for speeding, but other than that it was a smooth drive.

So, with the police radio on in the car, listening with detached curiosity to the workings of the Northern Constabulary, they were already almost back in Strathpeffer when the call came through from McLeod, looking for assistance at the house of the dead minister.

'Just in time,' said Crow, heading up the hill passed Kinnahaird.

'Not for the fella who's dead,' said Cameron.

Crow did not reply, but kicked the car down into second and gunned the accelerator, on their way past a field of sheep.

f

McLeod ran into the vicar's house, followed by McGowan, Igor and a strangely disinterested Barney. Here we go, he was thinking, another murder scene.

Into the sitting room, and immediately it was evident that the Reverend Wilson had been dead for some time. His body was slumped into the settee, his face was blue, and a great deal of blood had dried on his face and across his dressing gown. Just as the blood on the wall above the television, where the face of death had been crudely drawn, had dried dull and lacklustre. McLeod stopped and quickly assessed the room, the vague panic and indecisiveness in his head slowing down, now that he realised that he wasn't going to have to fight any serial killers or anything.

'Don't touch anything,' he said quickly to the others, looking round at them and doing a calming thing with his hands. Already regretting getting them to come along. Guaranteed one of them would touch something and he'd get his backside booted all over the shop by the Chief Constable and a variety of ranks in between.

Wasn't about to touch anything, thought Barney. And implicate myself in a murder? thought McGowan, no chance. I heard this guy had a cool selection of 11th Century Californian lithographs, thought Igor, I might just have a quick look around before the SOCO's get here.

There was a knock at the front door, there were a pair of contrasting footsteps, and then the sitting room door swung open. Presuming the reinforcements from Dingwall, McLeod turned round to be confronted by Earl Strathcaln and his wife, come to pay a visit to the Reverend Wilson on a matter of some embarrassment to the Earl.

Strathcaln stared at the curious scene, the four men and the vicar's body, his missus standing beside him dressed in tight fitting blue, an unwilling visitor.

'Bugger me up the arse with a lollipop,' said Strathcaln, 'what's this?'

'He's dead, Jim,' said McLeod. 'Murdered last night,

by the looks of it.'

'Bugger me sideways with a kettle,' Strathcaln added, still taken aback by the whole thing.

There was a knock at the door. Not the police, thought McLeod. Who else are we going to have join the fray?

'Come in!' he shouted, and immediately confident footsteps strode across the hall carpet.

Theodore Wolf's ugly mug appeared at the door of the sitting room. He stopped for a second, then immediately charged into the midst of the crowd, looking from one bystander to another, and checking out the corpse. He stood over Wilson's body for a few seconds, then turned to McLeod.

'This man's dead,' he said.

'Good spot,' said McLeod.

'Arf,' said Igor.

'It's going to be really tough to shift those stains,' said Wolf. 'What you need, is New Improved Domestic Stain-be-Gone. Just spray it on, and the stain is gone!'

They all stared at him. There's a time for marketing— although no one is really sure exactly when that is—and there's a time for marketing men to keep their gobs shut.

'Bad timing?' said Wolf.

'Why are you here?' countered McLeod.

'Thought I might sell the preacher some advice on how to improve the size of his throng, if you know what I'm saying.'

McLeod breathed deeply and turned to Strathcaln.

'And what are you doing here, your grace?'

'Had an appointment with his eminence here on a rather delicate matter.'

'Well,' said McLeod, 'he's dead, so you might just like to take your leave.'

'What are you doing letting us in, you bloody fool,' said Strathcaln. 'The wife here could be traumatised.'

Soo Yin was checking out the stiff with a detached interest. More traumatised, if the truth be known, by the sight of her husband in the buff. Which was fair enough.

'Back up hasn't arrived yet,' said McLeod. 'They'll be here in a minute, so if you'd all just like to take your leave, I can make sure the crime scene doesn't get contaminated.'

Once again there were footsteps outside, as more visitors came to call. Just to recap, in case anyone is getting confused, currently present were Barney Thomson, barber, Luke McGowan, barber, Igor, barber's assistant, Theodore Wolf, annoying person, Earl Strathcaln, landed gentry, Soo Yin Strathcaln, catalogue chick, Detective Sergeant McLeod, who was gradually losing control of the situation, and the very late Reverend Wilson, who was due to become a little pungent if not seen to with greater haste than was currently being employed.

The sitting room door was once again pushed open, and in walked Legal Attachés Crow and Cameron. They stopped and surveyed the unusually heavily populated scene.

'Crow,' said Crow, unnecessarily.

'Cameron,' said Lara Cameron. 'My family left Scotland in 1643.'

'Arf,' said Igor.

'Aye, aye,' said McLeod, expecting a rebuke, 'there's a weird set of circumstances here. These people were just leaving.'

'That's all right,' said Crow, 'the murderer is in this room, so we can sort it out while we're here.'

'Cool,' said Theodore Wolf. 'Just like Poirot or Scooby Doo or some shit like that.'

Barney raised an eyebrow, his heart beating a little faster. Nothing to say that these comedians wouldn't have discovered his identity and were drawing their own conclusions.

'In this room?' said McLeod. 'Oh my God!'

McGowan stared at the floor; Igor's hunch arched a little further; Strathcaln looked around the room suspiciously, Soo Yin bit her bottom lip; Wolf wondered if he might be able to advise the soon to be defendant on how to act in court.

'I'm making a bit of an assumption that the fella who killed the preacher here is the same one took out the students,' said Crow, and then noticing the drawing on the wall, 'but that seems to point to it, and it's hard to imagine a backwoods kinda place like this having more than one killer hanging around. We'll do the DNA shit and check it out.'

'So what's the story then?' said Strathcaln, not one for beating about the bush. 'Come on, man.'

Crow walked to the window, where he could better observe the group. Yep, he thought, this is a bit like Poirot, or one of those detective guys. And what the Hell, nothing wrong with a bit of showboating in front of the provincials. Cameron uncritically let him away with it, as she kept herself between the door and the suspect.

'Last Friday was a misty day round these parts, right?' said Crow, not looking for an answer. Had already checked his facts. 'Couldn't see further 'n about three feet. So, when the four student fellas went to get their hair cutting, not many folk saw them about town. Too damn thick with fog. So they all went to McGowan's here.'

'I never gave those cuts!' protested McGowan.

'Sure you didn't,' said Crow. 'You're shit, but you're not that shit. Thing is, you were somewhere else on Friday morning, when you'd normally have been working in the shop. Got a call that morning, didn't you?'

'No I didn't,' he said robustly, and Wolf was impressed with his outright denial of the facts when directly accused.

'Damn right you did, friend,' said Crow. 'You got a call from the Earl's wife here, didn't you? Went round to see her, didn't you?'

McGowan looked outraged. The Earl turned to his wife. 'Soo?'

She was a bit bug-eyed, but to give her her due, she didn't try and deny it.

'Good God, have you been having an affair?' said Strathcaln.

She didn't answer. McGowan looked a little sheepish, as the truth was being outed in front of a few more people than he would ideally have chosen.

'No affair, Your Bigness,' said Crow, 'he's been paying the chick for sex.'

'God!' shouted Strathcaln in an enormous ejaculation.

'And I'm telling you buddy, he's not the only one,' Crow added.

Strathcaln looked at her, his face bulging and red, which wasn't a very attractive sight.

McGowan started to explode into vehement denial, but well, you know, when faced with the truth, sometimes it's difficult to be too intense in your own defence. 'Bastard,' was all that ended up coming out.

'So you left the haircutting duties to Igor here,' said Crow, 'and it was this little fella who gave the four students their terrible cuts.'

'Arf,' said Igor. He wanted to proclaim his defence. He'd had no formal training; McGowan occasionally threw him in at the deep end with very little warning; the students had asked for bad hair.

Barney shook his head. Shocking behaviour to put the hair of innocent customers at risk like that. This was all passing him by, however, and he wished he'd just turned and taken the opportunity to walk away. Whoever was going to be pinned down as the murderer, it wasn't him. He might as well already be on his way to Inverness.

'So Igor killed the students?' said McLeod.

71

'Arf!'

'Nah,' said Crow, 'too simple. His part just explains the shit haircuts. To find the killer you have to go back to the night before, when they spent the evening in the bar of the Highland Inn. They talked to a variety of people. Ad man here, with all his bullshit, the barbers, that bar guy who keeps telling everybody he drinks his own urine. Hell, a lot of others as well. And on top of all that, one of those students spoke to her ladyship here, or whatever she's called. The Thai catalogue chick. That not right?' said Crow.

Soo Yin backed off a little, but it was only in the direction of the door, where Cameron waited to catch the killer.

'So what?' boomed Strathcaln, getting a bit lost by the whole thing. 'They talked to everyone. Social little bastards, that's what I called them.'

'Thing was,' said Crow, 'that they found something out about your little mail order princess here, didn't they?'

Strathcaln was stopped in his boots. He knew what was coming, having been to see the vicar this day to discuss the very same matter. Barney looked on, thinking that here was confirmation of his suspicions. Funny sometimes, how things fall into place.

'I'm lost,' said McLeod.

'The princess here,' said Crow, 'is more of a prince, you know what I'm saying?'

He smiled. McLeod swallowed and looked at her. It wasn't like he was some provincial clown who didn't know such things happened, he'd just never thought. Soo Yin was pretty damn hot, after all.

Luke McGowan, however, was about to be sick.

'What?' he croaked.

Strathcaln was silent, having discovered the truth a few weeks previously.

'I've had the operation!' squealed Soo Yin, threatening

72

to throw a tantrum.

'Your girlfriend here,' said Crow to McGowan, 'is a katoey. She was born a man, and at some stage she's had the old snipperoo, you get me? We went down to the Thai consulate today, checked out a few things about her. Bit of a past as well, eh, princess?'

The breath caught in McGowan's throat. Things like this didn't happen in Strathpeffer. He was going to be the laughing stock of the entire town. Already, Theodore Wolf was laughing.

'Very good, Agent Crow,' said Strathcaln, 'but it doesn't make her a murderer.'

'Come on,' said Crow, 'one of the students picked her. They'd been in Bangkok recently, they knew the score. She was scared they'd let her secret out. Hell, maybe they threatened to blackmail her. So she killed 'em. You want to take her in, Sergeant, get the samples, you know they're going to match."

'Soo Yin?' said Strathcaln, turning to his wife.

Discovering that your wife is a prostitute and a murderer at the same time is a bit of a shock. Good thing he already knew she'd been a man.

'It's preposterous,' she said, looking around for some implement or other that she could use to murder everyone in the room.

'What about the vicar?' said McLeod.

'Hell, who knows?' said Crow. 'Catalogue Girl here probably had some reason or other for wanting rid of him.'

'Stop calling me that!' she snapped at Crow. 'He refused to pay me. Twice, the bastard. He deserved everything he got.'

'Soo!' said Strathcaln, beginning to be a bit devastated, to be honest.

Soo Yin had already checked out the door, and the

impediment of Agent Cameron. Acting quickly, she grabbed the nearest implement to hand—a large brass sculpture of Sandy Lyle winning the '87 Masters, very handy for bashing people over the head—and swung viciously before her as she headed for the door.

Cameron ducked and expertly caught Soo Yin with a punch to the guts, a brutal blow which brought her to her knees, and she collapsed on the floor with a grunting eruption of breath, dropping Sandy Lyle in the process. Cameron stood over her, while the rest of the audience looked on in horror/amusement/revulsion/curiosity, depending on who they were.

'I'm finished in this town,' said McGowan wretchedly.

'You're shite at cutting hair anyway,' said Barney, deciding to dole out a home truth.

Strathcaln stared down at his wife. Today he'd hoped to clear his conscience about the sex change thing with the Reverend Wilson. No wonder Soo Yin had been so against going.

'There's more to it, James,' she said desperately, looking up at him. 'Much more.'

Such as how a wee woman like her had managed to murder four strapping students, and how she'd got hold of Igor's scissors.

He hesitated, but he did not care to know what the rest of the story might be. His was the real disgrace, not McGowan or anyone else who might have slept with his wife. He reached inside his pocket where he kept the, until now, pointless little handgun that he carried everywhere with him. Crow and Cameron both saw the movement, but they weren't expecting it, not here. With one smooth movement, as if he had been waiting all his life for the moment, he brought out the gun, shot Soo Yin with one perfectly aimed bullet in the forehead, then turned it on himself and blasted off the back

74

of his head before anyone could make a move to stop him.

The blood from Strathcaln's head exploded over the room, catching the jackets of both Igor and Theodore Wolf, then his body collapsed in a great thudding heap against the sofa.

Soo Yin lay dead on the floor, face upturned, dead eyes open; the eyes that had once looked upon the world as a man.

The others had all taken a step back at the explosive end to this little drama of revelation, and immediately Crow felt regret at creating the artificial scene which had allowed Strachcaln to murder his wife before they'd had a chance to gather all the facts.

'Arf,' said Igor as a fitting epitaph.

And man that's all she wrote.

Epilogue

A Beginning

"A tower of nine storeys begins with a heap of earth.
The journey of a thousand li starts from where one stands.
Breakfast begins with a plate of honey loops."
Lao Tzu (604-531BC)

The police arrived in force almost immediately after, thirty strong, but the drama was over. Barney hung around in the throng of people for a while, one of many, waiting for his chance to get out of Dodge. He was briefly interviewed by a constable from Dingwall, and then he was released to the masses.

As he was walking slowly from the house he came across Legal Attaché Lara Cameron, standing by the door. One last chat, one last aimless dance around the issue of vague attraction.

'You off?' she said, as he passed her by.

'Aye,' said Barney, stopping.

'Where to?' she said.

Barney looked out at the cold grey afternoon.

'Don't know,' he said. 'Inverness probably.'

'What'll you do?'

'Not sure,' he replied. 'Sometimes you just have to bite the antelope on the arse.'

'Right,' she said.

They looked at each other, one last time, and Barney nodded and walked from the house, feeling her eyes on the back of his head. And then he was out into the crowd that had gathered outside the old manse, and he was lost from view.

And off he walked along the road, his bag slung over his shoulder. As itinerant as Theodore Wolf, but with a lot less money.

f

Later that afternoon, Damien Crow returned to the Touchstone Maze. He spent three hours searching for something, the nature of which he would only know when he found it. The dark had long arrived, and he was moving from stone to stone with a large torch, when he finally came across what he was looking for.

In the thirteenth stone starting from the centre of the circle, a folded granite gneiss, there was a hole, a few inches across, which ran through the side of the rock. And deep inside the hole, pushed up against the stone so that only the most exacting of searches could have uncovered it, he found a tiny piece of paper.

He had great trouble dislodging it, even after he had discovered its existence, in the end having to carefully use a small branch collected from the forest.

Once retrieved he held the piece of paper between his thumb and forefinger and shone the torch upon it. It was square, barely a quarter of a centimetre across, the paper yellowed by time. So small, that there was only space for one character, hand written in blue ink;

✱

He pulled a small plastic bag from his pocket and carefully placed the paper inside. He switched off the torch, looked around at the cold forest in the dark of an early evening in the Highlands of Scotland in winter, then turned and began the walk back down into the town.